AF302177

Claudia Haase

A Date with Castle Ruins

Bibliografische Information der Deutschen Nationalbibliothek / Bibliographic Information of the German National Library:
Die Deutsche Nationalbibliothek verzeichnet diese Publikation in der Deutschen Nationalbibliografie; detaillierte bibliografische Daten sind im Internet über http://dnb.dnb.de abrufbar / The German National Library lists this publication in the Deutsche Nationalbibliografie; detailed bibliographic data are available on the internet at http://dnb.dnb.de

Edited by Sierra Campbell – Editing by Sierra

Production and publishing:
BoD – Books on Demand, Norderstedt

Cover: Comet #21892, BookCoverZone.com, Design by Diren Yardimli

ISBN: 978-3-7578-8794-0

Table of Contents

CHAPTER 1 – ANTICIPATION 9

CHAPTER 2 – MICE COURT HOUSE......................... 13

CHAPTER 3 – OTHER PLANS 19

CHAPTER 4 – GOODBYE VACATION 26

CHAPTER 5 – NO DAYLIGHT 31

CHAPTER 6 – PLAN B... 33

CHAPTER 7 – AN OWL OR A GHOST? 41

CHAPTER 8 - TROUBLEMAKERS 49

CHAPTER 9 – A DREAM OR FORESHADOWING? . 51

CHAPTER 10 - CAUGHT 53

CHAPTER 11 - JEALOUSY.. 60

CHAPTER 12 – THE VERDICT....................................... 68

CHAPTER 13 – MOSAIC BRICKS 75

CHAPTER 14 – GUESSING GAME 78

CHAPTER 15 – DAMN GENEROUS 80

ACKNOWLEDGEMENT 91

ALSO BY CLAUDIA HAASE....................................... 92

CHAPTER 1 – ANTICIPATION

It was bone-chillingly cold, but the sun shone down from the sky with all its might and enveloped the old ruins of Sturmstein Castle in glistening light. Babsi happily enjoyed the morning walk with her wife Theodora. It was not often that she could be persuaded to leave work and go for a walk. Especially not in the snow-covered Citadel Park that is right outside of the city. Her attempts to avoid it still rang in Babsi's ears: "I'd rather relax at home. Do you really want to drive in this weather?"

But somehow, she had gotten Theodora out of the door. The walk through the park put her in good spirits for the approaching Christmas season. Before the holidays, they would spend their first vacation together with their daughter, Hannah. Babsi was looking forward to exploring the snowy area around Bergtels Village with her two sweethearts.

Over the past year and a half that Babsi and Theodora had been a couple, there has been a lack of occasions for a trip. After their wedding a few months ago, they had planned and longed for their first summer vacation together, which they had to postpone again and again and finally cancel.

It had been Theodora's suggestion to go to Bergfels and visit Bergfels Palace and the famous Christmas Market. She had wanted to report on the market while they were there.

Who knows if Hannah will travel with us without grumbling in the next few years, Babsi thought. Soon, her almost 15-year-old daughter would surely prefer to go on trips with her girlfriends.

Babsi looked over at Sturmstein Castle. It certainly couldn't compete with the palace of her vacation spot, but the thick, partly caved-in walls still provided an impressive setting. The icicles hanging in front of the wall openings looked like curtain tips, and made the masonry look inviting and cozy.

For a moment, Babsi imagined what it would be like to sit at a richly set table inside the vault. She dreamed of a hall brightly lit by candles with melodic harp music in the background. Sighing, she snuggled up to Theodora's warm cashmere coat.

"It's a wonder that Sturmstein Castle hasn't been flattened yet so that a real estate tycoon or grasshopper investors can build apartments on the property," Babsi marveled. "The view from here over the park and the city is phenomenal, isn't it? They could charge rents..."

"It is only a castle ruin and not a well-preserved castle. The property probably belongs to several people, making the ownership unclear," Theodora guessed.

"I wonder if any kings or princes lived in it before." Babsi hummed thoughtfully. "Maybe it belongs to the descendants of a German emperor?"

"I don't think so. In that case, I'm sure there would be a museum or an archive there and the structure wouldn't be in such disrepair."

"Too bad it's not occupied." Babsi laughed briefly and stopped. Theodora looked at her questioningly.

"My grandma used to tell me that the ghost of a princess lived there and wrote love letters every night, lamenting her suffering. After her accidental death in the nearby river, the princess returned to the castle as a ghost. And during her writing breaks, she supposedly preys on curious little children."

"How creepy. Not very responsible of your grandmother to tell you this."

"Oh, my grandma only said this to prevent us from sneaking to the ruin. Of course, we were insanely curious, but didn't dare to go and play there. We were afraid and actually believed that the ghost of a princess or others lived there. When we rode our bicycles, we stopped far away and wondered what was going on behind the walls."

Babsi absorbed the sight of the ruin. "Yet it lies there so peaceful and abandoned. There was certainly no drama going on behind those walls. Otherwise, the public would have noticed."

CHAPTER 2 – MICE COURT HOUSE

"The defendant, mouse Murina, is accused of going to the office of the *Lesbian Line*, a telephone counselling service in the *Recreational Center for Girls and Young Women,* in the pre-Christmas period last year and stealing a lottery ticket, as well as transporting it outside the office into a wastepaper box."

Murina looked down at the ground. She wished that her friend—Athena, who is an owl—could make herself small enough to join her in the depths of the ruins of Sturmstein Castle. Both to stand by her and to explain the whole incident in her always calm and thoughtful way. Especially since this incident was almost one year ago and she had almost forgotten it.

Why, only now? Was there not a limit on how long it could be before she couldn't be charged? Murina remembered with a shudder how the mouse police had picked her up in the garden of the *Recreational Center for Girls and Young Women* two days ago. Paralyzed by the shock, she had only dimly remembered the way to the old castle ruins, in the basement of which the mouse prison and the court were located.

"Witness Sori observed the defendant do this and recorded the course of events in detail. By doing so, the defendant has violated section 15 paragraph 2 CCM, Civil Code of Mice," Judge Arvalis announced in a stern voice.

"Objection, Your Honor!" Murina wanted to shout. But she had to admit that it had happened that way. She had almost slipped on the lottery ticket during one of her walks through the office. Neat and tidy as she was, she had dragged the paper to the trash can and thrown it in. Stupidly, she hadn't noticed Sori, who must have been hiding in the hole in the wall like an informer.

Sori and her family clan belonged to the shrews, equipped with pointed noses to sniff around. In the time before her arrest, she had often run into Sori and her evil pack, and they always had nasty things to say.

Sori even said that Murina, as a refugee from the country, had no right to enter the *Recreational Center for Girls and Young Women*. But the whole thing belonged to the people and not to the shrews.

Thanks to her clever cellmate, Murina knew by now that Section 15(2) of the CCM allowed the nibbling or moving of small objects that belonged to people but punished the carrying of things to other rooms.

Murina would have liked to run away. Not that she was afraid of Judge Arvalis. With her impressive appearance, plump body, small ears, and short tail, she looked like Murina's grandmother. Granny had been strict, too—as strict as Judge Arvalis—but had had a big heart. She hoped the same was true for the jurist. But Murina had never attended a court hearing, especially when she was the reason for the hearing.

Meanwhile, Sori sat with a smug smile in the front row of the crowd of mice, flanked by two companions who nibbled on a piece of earthworm without a second thought. *They weren't in the mouse cinema after all!*

"Well, Murina, what do you have to say in your defense?" the judge asked.

"Your Honor," Murina began stammering, "I just wanted to get the chit of paper out of the way because I almost slipped on it."

"So, you admit to the crime?"

"Yes, but ..." she began, but Sori and her friends burst into loud cheers and Murina's voice died.

The audience in the courtroom shouted wildly.

"Look, she admits it!"

"She should be locked up!"

"Clearly, this Old World mouse has committed a crime!"

Murina couldn't make a sound. Yet it was so important to clear up the matter. In the end, despite Murina's intervention, the visitors of the *Recreational Center for Girls and Young Women* had not been harmed at all. They would never be harmed by Murina!

"Quiet!" Arvalis knocked on the table.

"Ahem," Murina's public defender spoke up. She had been forcibly assigned to her, because Murina had no savings to afford her own lawyer.

"I ask for mercy on behalf of my client and would like to emphasize that as a refugee from the country, she does not have a home of her own or a thick cheese reservoir in order to buy one. Nor is she familiar with the local conditions and regulations."

Murina was thrilled by the public defender's efforts—*what a professional!* She raised her front paws to clap but lowered them when she noticed her lawyer's threatening glances.

Last winter she would definitely have frozen to death if Athena hadn't allowed her to slip under her warm feathers from time to time at night. And she would have starved to death if the young women in the *Recreational Center for Girls and Young Women* hadn't graciously left some cheese or cracker crumbs lying around from time to time.

"Or how do you see it?"

Murina winced. She had drifted off and had not heard the judge's question.

"It is unclear to me how the trash can is not considered part of the office," Arvalis repeated, as if she had noticed Murina's mental absence. "After all, people seem to throw paper in there, which is part of the office routine of humans, among other things. I don't want to jump to conclusions, so I'm ordering a crime scene review at the center. The hearing is adjourned until after the site visit."

"This is outrageous, she should be behind bars forever! She has violated the mice law!"

"A committal is absolutely unnecessary, she has confessed!"

Desperate insults came from Sori's supporters, and the burly police-mice had trouble keeping them away from Murina and the judge.

But Murina did not mind. She could have jumped with joy. She smiled gratefully at Arvalis. She was already looking forward to finally being able to leave this dark building.

She lost her sparkle, however, when the judge added, "And the defendant will remain in custody until then. Since she is known to have no fixed abode, she is a flight risk."

The audience of mice booed and cheered at the same time, but Sori's shout was the loudest. "We don't want to run into Murina in the rec center again. That belongs to us shrews!"

Before Murina knew what was happening, two of the mouse cops were hooking her arms, and she couldn't scoot along fast enough to keep up with them. The law enforcement officers carried her out of the courtroom and through the hall back to the prison wing.

CHAPTER 3 – OTHER PLANS

"Didn't you understand my question?" It resounded through the telephone. Lost in reverie, Countess Flordelis Mathilde Ida of Bergfels-Blumenheide, known only as Ida to her close confidants and friends, looked out the window, watching the snowflakes gently falling down. How long had it been since she had taken out her cross-country skis and glided through the white, untouched landscape?

"Ida, you still on the line?" asked Theodora.

"Sorry, I was distracted. Now I'm all ears," Ida affirmed.

"I just wanted to know when you would be setting up for the Christmas Market. I thought I'd stop by Bergfels for a long weekend with Babsi and Hannah. For a story. Babsi is already giddy with excitement."

The Christmas Market in front of Bergfels Palace, which belonged to Ida's family, was very popular and known far beyond the borders of the community. Her father had urged Ida and her brother to help set up the stalls and decorate them when they were children—free of charge, of course.

As a reward, they had been given a warm cocoa on opening day and had been allowed to choose a carved toy or knitted socks from the stalls.

"So far my boss has rejected the proposal. Don't you remember? To him, Bergfels is a backwater town and would be laughable in our magazine. He doesn't think it would drive up circulation," Theodora explained.

"Yes, how could I forget? We even sent him some promotional stuff through the palace's administration that contained information about the pre-Christmas events," Ida interjected.

"Well, I guess that helped. Anyway, now he thinks there's a trend toward smaller Christmas markets coming up, and a report on yours would be just right."

"Theodora, I'm sorry to disappoint you. But nothing of the sort will take place here this year." Ida rubbed her eyes. "We have other plans."

"Oh." That was all Theodora could say, and Ida could see the disappointment on her friend's face, despite only being on the phone.

"For three years now, the supermarket in the neighboring town has been putting on this commercial Christmas Market, with loud bling-

bling LEDs, cheap plastic items, and mulled wine stands, along with roaring live music. We can't keep up with that with our stalls; there are just fewer visitors."

"Such nonsense." Theodora sounded indignant.

"However, I can kind of understand. Everyone around here has enough handmade Christmas items and knitted goods at home. But we've decided to exhibit only handmade things and sell homemade punch and fruit cake. We don't want to do without that—that's what made it so appealing."

"I couldn't imagine anything more beautiful. That's exactly what's missing in our town, apart from the volunteer-organized bazaars," Theodora remarked, and a hint of longing resonated through the phone.

"If my father could hear you talk like this! He incessantly says it's tradition and insists it stays that way. He'd rather accept cancelling the Christmas Market than making changes to the handmade items. Of course, the shindig that is organized in the neighboring village is something different. Listening to the children's choir sing *Silent Night* is not exactly a hit, especially since the voices can hardly compete with an enormous choir from a city. And they certainly can't be compared to live background music by professional artists."

"I'll tell you what—we'll come over anyway. Then Babsi can finally meet you and Charlotte. Hannah will be amazed when she sees Bergfels Palace for the first time. The two of them don't know yet that, purely by chance, the Count's daughter is one of my best friends. They think you're just working for a Children's Aid Organization." Ida could literally hear Theodora's grin through the line. "Do you have snow, too?"

"Of course we have! Yesterday it was still fifty centimeters."

"Oh, it hasn't snowed much here yet. We could do some hiking and take our skis with us. We can still stay with you, right?"

"Uh, I'm really busy right now, and I'll be on the road constantly for the next few weeks." Ida didn't believe the excuse herself, so she had to give her excuse a little more weight. "Of course, you can still sleep here, but we wouldn't see each other. Besides, all of the heaters in the guest rooms are being serviced at the moment."

Ida could have kicked herself. Who, pray tell, maintained heaters in the middle of winter? But she did not want to tell Theodora about her plans now. Although she had canceled the Christmas Market in front of the palace, that didn't mean it couldn't be held elsewhere.

Her wife, Charlotte, had found out in the Count's archives that the castle ruins, which were enthroned at the gates of Theodora's hometown, belonged to the Count's family.

Now the plan had grown to organize a Christmas Market in front of the remains of Sturmstein Castle. However, she wanted to keep her plans a secret from Theodora as long as possible; the whole thing was supposed to be a surprise for her best friend. Moreover, she wanted to commission experts to assess the possibility and costs of securing, renovating, and maintaining the old ruin walls.

"Charlotte and I will be spending most of our time in my city apartment for the next few weeks; the infrastructure is just better there, the airport is faster to get to, and the Internet is more reliable," she added for good measure.

"What a shame." Theodora sighed. "But it wouldn't be half as nice without you and Charlotte. And we don't want to freeze, either."

"We'll put it off until next year." Ida tried to let mused enthusiasm come through. "I'll block out the last weekend before Christmas on the calendar and then the three of you can come over."

"That's what we can do!" agreed Theodora. "I've already put it down."

"Then, perhaps, it will be time for a Christmas Market in front of the palace again, but I don't want to promise anything."

"Anyway, Bergfels is worth a trip that way, too. But maybe we can meet after the holidays when you're a little less stressed? Honestly, waiting a whole year for a reunion is too long for me."

"Let's talk more some other time, okay? I have an important meeting with the administrator of our estates in a minute."

Ida quickly ended the call. Her eyes fell on the thick folder in front of her, emblazoned in black letters with *Christmas Market at the ruins of Sturmstein Castle.*

She rubbed her hands together. Organizing the market in a completely different, new location brought back the anticipation she had lost in recent years when planning. The city council had already approved the event and involved the municipal authority responsible for regulating public events in the planning.

Ida had promised to donate part of the proceeds to charity institutions for children and young adults in the city, and her father, Count of Bergfels-Blumenheide, would give the opening speech in person.

In return, she had requested the strictest secrecy from the city council until at least the construction of the booths was completed and her plan could no longer be concealed.

Since the project promised good publicity for the city, the mayor committed all those charged with the organization to silence and secrecy.

Now all Ida had to do was convince Theodora's boss that the Christmas Market belonged on the front page of *City Culture.* And, of course, his most capable editor had to cover the event—Theodora Nachtweih herself.

CHAPTER 4 – GOODBYE VACATION

I should have known better. Of course, once again something comes up. Fate wants us to postpone this short trip as well. Goodbye vacation.

Disappointed, Babsi looked at the walnut cookies in the oven that were slowly turning a goldish-brown color. After learning that both the Christmas Market and the extended weekend in Bergfels would not take place, she had fled to Theodora's high-tech kitchen in a rage and set about baking. Hannah had practically devoured the homemade cookies from Theodora's grandma's recipe last year. *Who knows when my wife will get around to baking with her workload.*

During the short trip, she had wanted to suggest to her wife that they finally merge their households completely and rent out one of the two apartments in the house. They spent most of their time in Babsi's apartment upstairs, and Theodora only used her study and rarely the luxuriously furnished living room downstairs.

In Babsi's eyes, this was a pure waste of living space. Not to mention the money they would make by renting it out. They could have the country stove with the grill and two ovens brought upstairs—she didn't want to give that back. Cookies and cakes really tasted better when baked with it.

"Mom?" called Hannah from upstairs, coming down the stairs. "There you are! Whoa, that smells good, are they almost done?" She peered over Babsi's shoulder. "By the way, Theodora said you were mad at her. But it's not her fault that her friend couldn't organize the Christmas Market."

Babsi sighed. *At least Theodora told our daughter that the trip would not take place—that way I will be spared.* Apparently, Hannah took it well.

"It doesn't matter," her daughter continued. "The long drive wouldn't have been worth it for a weekend anyway. By the way, I found an alternate event for Theodora."

"Did you?" Curious, Babsi leaned against the kitchen counter and gave Hannah her full attention.

"She's going to report on our Christmas bazaar at the *Recreational Center for Girls and Young Women.* Anyway, that's what she's going to suggest to her boss."

"You're talking about your little volunteer bazaar? Do you seriously think that's a good substitute for the Christmas Market in front of a real palace?"

Babsi had to refrain from laughing out loud. She bit her tongue to save herself from further comments. "Sorry, but that's too funny," she snorted.

"You won't be laughing when Nele and I are grinning at you from the cover of Theodora's magazine," Hannah countered. "With our homemade knitted rainbow hats on our heads!" She glared angrily at her mother.

"It's not Theodora's magazine, and she certainly doesn't get to decide who gets photographed on the cover."

"Geez, Ma, you're such a buzzkill! Of course, we don't get to decide."

"I don't think her boss will go for it. Don't get your hopes up, then you won't be too disappointed if he doesn't." Babsi tried to curb her daughter's eagerness.

"He is." Theodora had joined them unnoticed. "He has just agreed to my plan B. I explained to him that the bazaar is a different kind of pre-Christmas event. It shows that, away from the big commercial markets, there are still non-profit events put on by volunteers."

"And that one argument was enough for him to sign off on it?" asked Babsi in amazement. She had completely misjudged Theodora's boss so far.

"No. That was first." Theodora used her fingers to list additional points. "Secondly, all the other Christmas markets in our city are flooded in droves by the regional reporters from our daily newspapers, so our magazine doesn't even need to get involved." Theodora stopped, looked up at her, and waited for her to agree. "Isn't that right?"

Babsi smiled and nodded appreciatively at her wife. "And third?"

"Third, it's a great way to point out the colorful and diverse side of our city and introduce the readership to the *Recreational Center for Girls and Young Women* and the work of those involved there."

"We could print the center's donation account under the report," Hannah suggested. Babsi winced at the *we.* Her daughter probably already saw herself as a co-reporter.

But Theodora didn't seem to mind at all. "A dazzling idea," she agreed. "Maybe this way you'll still come into a little money for your activities."

A little publicity couldn't hurt the center, which was always short on cash. *On closer inspection, Hannah's idea is not so bad,* Babsi had to admit to herself.

"Thealein, Hannah, I'm proud of you!" She really was proud of her loved ones and could not restrain herself from calling Theodora by the nickname she always objected.

The oven beeped and Babsi took out the tray with the steaming cookies. As soon as she put it down, Theodora and Hannah tried to nibble on the cookies.

"Are you girls crazy? It's still way too hot. And if you eat it all now, we won't have anything for Christmas." She stood in front of the baking tray and put her hands on her hips. "You better help me shape the rest of the dough into cookies."

Surprisingly, the two followed her request without a murmur.

CHAPTER 5 – NO DAYLIGHT

The small cave in the mouse prison, where Murina had been in custody for several days, was anything but cozy. She was freezing and the floor was muddy, with water seeping in from somewhere. Nevertheless, there was no crack in the walls that would have let daylight into this lower part of the castle ruins.

Every few hours, the guard mice threw moldy breadcrumbs into her cell, which Murina shared with her cellmate Sylva, a wood mouse.

Most of the time she dozed off, half asleep, dreaming of her owl friend Athena and reminiscing about the good times she had with her.

She also missed her quick visits to the *Recreational Center for Girls and Young Women,* where she loved to watch as they made plans and organized events. If she stayed here any longer, she would miss the Christmas bazaar that was held there every year.

There were delicious smelling waffles and some crumbles always fell on the ground. She would even miss the Christmas carols that the girls and women sang and that sounded crooked and lopsided in her mouse ears.

She suppressed a sob and quickly wiped a tear from her cheek. She didn't want her cellmate to see how much she was suffering.

"Hey, do you hear that too?" Sylva's words snapped her out of her self-pity. Murina raised her head and listened intently. What was going on in front of the castle ruins? Car noises, then objects being thumped on the ground, followed by hammering, drilling, and sawing. Men's voices were shouting wildly.

"I wish I could see something. What's happening? What are the people up to?" complained Sylva a little too loudly.

"Quiet!" one of the guard mice yelled through the hallway.

Couldn't the people use their tools purely by chance to knock a hole diagonally through the ground and create an escape route? Hope sprouted in Murina. If she only squealed loudly enough, Athena would come to her rescue, grab her with her fangs, and take her far away from this terrible place and to safety.

CHAPTER 6 – PLAN B

Theodora pulled her head in, tugged the cashmere scarf around her neck a little higher, and tried to make herself as small as possible. Hannah and her friends Emilia, Laura, and Nele walked down the narrow street in front of them, giggling and chatting eagerly. Hopefully no one recognized them. After all, they lived only a few streets away and the teenagers were making quite a racket.

"Shh! Do you have to be so loud? People will complain about the noise." But the girls ignored her.

Laughing, Babsi hooked arms with her. "Oh, Thealein, they're already used to it. Besides, most houses are shared by students. They make just as much noise. Didn't you ever walk around talking loudly with your friends?" she wondered. "They're just in high spirits this close to the Christmas bazaar. You'll be amazed at what ideas they have!"

Theodora regretted that she had made the photo series about the bazaar in the center palatable to her boss. But there was no turning back. For a few days now, he had been excited for the proposal and obsessed with the idea that the articles in the *City Culture* magazine needed to be more diverse.

The decisive factor for him was to attract as many new subscribers as possible. Certainly, he was not really interested in showing the diversity, colorfulness, and tolerance of the city. Nor would he permanently include relevant articles in his magazine.

"Once we've gained new subscribers, we'll quickly return to serious reporting," he had said. What was unserious about a report on their Christmas bazaar or, for instance, on a charity event at the Center for Queer People was beyond Theodora. Yet she was afraid that her article would not receive good feedback from the readership and the sales figures would not skyrocket. Then, her boss would never get involved with her suggestions again.

"You wouldn't believe how much I'm looking forward to it. It's a great opportunity for you to combine your professional and personal life," Babsi whispered to her. "Do you have any idea where you're going to start taking pictures?"

Babsi had advised her to take a quiet look around the halls of the center a few days before the bazaar. On the day of the event, it would be very crowded. Now, however, Theodora was able to take a few photos of the stalls, most of which were already prepared, without being disturbed.

All conceivable handicrafts, ceramics, self-made calendars, and many other beautiful things readily lay on lovingly decorated tables, as Hannah had told her at breakfast.

"I would like to have a look at the rest of the center and take some photos. But that depends on the lighting; daylight would have been better." Theodora was annoyed that she was busy the whole day and could only come in the evening.

Babsi sighed and adjusted her pom pom beanie. "It wasn't up to me. I was home on time after work."

"I know," Theodora admitted. "But I had an important phone call with our London branch, so I couldn't just hang up."

"Well, that's just the way it is. But I think the other rooms are locked at this hour. Only the great hall is accessible to us."

"Normally, yes. But Luna, one of the volunteers from the *Lesbian Line,* told me that she had given Hannah a master key to the other rooms. I'm allowed to look everywhere, and I've already thought of a few photo opportunities. Of course, on bazaar day, I'll ask one or two of the honorary women to pose for a photo in the rooms. Luna talks to the other women and girls and together they choose a few volunteers who don't mind seeing their picture in the press."

"Where are you guys?" Hannah jingled her keys. "We're freezing our butts off here. Come on, quick! We have to lock the door behind us, as I promised Luna."

"We're coming," Babsi grumbled into her scarf. Theodora walked quickly toward the *Recreational Center for Girls and Young Women*, pulling her wife along with her.

Hannah unlocked the door and the girls rushed in.

"Eh, let me go first!"

"Stop pushing!"

"Sorry, I can't see."

"Me neither."

"Geez, Hannah, turn on the lights!"

"May we come in, too?" Theodora made her presence known. "I'd like a little lighting, too, by the way."

"Shit," Hannah cursed. "It's not working."

"What? Nonsense, let me try," said one of her friends.

"Ouch, who's stepping on my foot?"

"Now stop the fun." Babsi snorted. "Theodora and I could spend the evening differently than listening to your sparring. Now turn on the lights!"

"It really doesn't work."

"Where's the switch?" inquired Theodora. "Would someone shine a flashlight down the hall?"

"Uh." Hannah sounded confused. "I do not have a flashlight!"

"You have a phone, don't you?" Theodora countered. "That icon with the lightbulb on it."

"Oh, I hadn't thought about that."

Finally, two of the girls held up their phones and aimed them at the light switch. Theodora pressed and pressed, but nothing happened.

"Come on, let's move along. Maybe it's just the light bulb that's broken." Hannah lit the way with her device. "There's a new bulb in the kitchen. I happened to be there when it was replaced. It'll definitely work." She strode ahead and the others sneaked behind.

Hannah reached through the doorway and a repeated clack filled the kitchen. But nothing.

"Crap, nothing works here either. Wait, I'll check upstairs. Laura, are you coming?"

"Sure. We just have to be careful not to step on the mouse's little paws."

"Mouse?" Babsi took a leap and bumped into Theodora, who inevitably grinned and bit her lips to keep from bursting out laughing. Her down-to-earth wife, who was too happy to let off steam in the garden, was scared of small creatures.

"There's a mouse here?"

"Yes, Mom, I told you. She's always fed cheese and crackers and she's totally cute. Something happened last year, you wouldn't believe..."

"You can tell us about the mouse and the lottery ticket later, now let's go and have a look," Laura urged.

Babsi shook herself. "Be careful and watch out!" The clatter of feet and giggles of the girls on the stairs moved away.

"Are you freezing?" Theodora felt Babsi shivering at her side. Was it the mouse or was she really shivering?

"Oh, the whole way I wasn't cold at all. But you must admit: Here in the dark, cold hall, the center looks really creepy. And when I imagine that some creature might run over my feet..." She clung to Theodora and gazed uncertainly into the darkness.

To them, it seemed as if they were waiting an eternity for Hannah and Laura. Emilia and Nele didn't seem to mind, though. They were playing with their phones and seemed to have forgotten everything around them, as Theodora noticed, not without a touch of envy.

At last, they heard footsteps and the voices of the returning girls.

"The power seems to be out all over the center," Laura announced.

"Yes, not only are the lights dead, but so is the refrigerator in the kitchen and the clock on the oven." Hannah's disappointment could not be overheard. "Do you know where the fuse box is?" Theodora's question earned nothing but perplexed looks and silence. "Shine a light on the walls and let me have a look." But her search was fruitless.

"It seems there's nothing that can be done about it," Hannah stated unnecessarily. "Now what?"

"Let's go home." Babsi hunched her shoulders. "Then you notify Luna, so she doesn't get a scare tomorrow when she comes in."

"Oh my, she's going to be dumbfounded!"

"Maybe it's just the fuse," Theodora tried to comfort the girls. "Or a small defect somewhere in the line. I'm sure an electrician can fix that." She swallowed her displeasure.

Plan B was now on the rocks. Hopefully they could get a grip on it quickly. If the Christmas bazaar couldn't take place, this story would also be history.

Holding it only by candlelight would certainly not be an option! Would candlelight even be allowed for fire safety reasons?

The possibilities to report on other pre-Christmas events were limited. At the same time, she didn't want to join the mediocre coverage of the major newspapers, which all wrote about the same markets.

CHAPTER 7 – AN OWL OR A GHOST?

Murina was outraged by the rumors that were circulating around the prison grounds. The rumor spread like wildfire that the electrical cables in the *Recreational Center for Girls and Young Women* had been cut. The culprits were allegedly mice. Furious, Murina kicked a small stone that almost jumped at the feet of one of the mouse guards who watched over the inmates on their daily rounds in the courtyard of the ruins.

Oh, if only I could talk to Athena and ask her if she observed anything from her branch in front of the center! Murina looked up at the towers of the ruin. Something was moving there among the old stones. An owl? No, she must have been wrong — she was seeing ghosts, clearly. It was due to her confinement. Especially since her cellmate constantly told her about some monsters that she encountered in her dreams.

Stop, stop! Murina was not mistaken. It almost took her breath away when she caught sight of Athena's big round eyes between the stones of the tower. Murina was bouncing on her toes with excitement.

She had to distract the guard so she could talk to Athena. But how? Keep the overseer at bay and talk to her friend at the same time? She couldn't. Blimey! Frustrated, she hung her head.

Suddenly, a murmur went through the whole group of mice, and everyone looked up. There! Her owl friend flew around in the air and emitted a loud, *huh-huh-huh* before opening her fangs and dropping several insects varying in size into the courtyard. Right at the feet of the guard.

Everyone sprang at the treats, the overseer pouncing first. Murina's heart pounded loudly. A great idea—she could rely on her friend!

"Huu-hu-huhuhuu," it sounded softly from the far corner of the yard. "Come to me, fast!"

Like a whirlwind, Murina ran to her friend.

"What a brilliant plan! You're just in time. I can't stand it here anymore. Will you take me with you?" Excitedly, she scurried around Athena.

"No, you know I can't do that. When it becomes public, then I'll have to stand trial at the Owl Court. After all, mice are at the top of our menu!"

"I thought we were friends!" Murina gasped in fright and jumped backwards.

"You're an exception, of course," Athena quickly affirmed, giving Murina a gentle pat on the head with her wing. "But listen to what I found out. The Christmas bazaar at the *Recreational Center for Girls and Young Women* can't take place. The electrical lines are chewed up and it will take weeks to repair."

"I heard about the accident and I'm just glad that I'm sitting here in custody, otherwise the judge might hold me responsible for that, too!" Murina said indignantly. "The poor women and girls, they always try so hard. Who would do that?"

"I think they are the same ones who betrayed you. There is a plot behind it. The evildoers surely want to take over the building so people can't use it. I heard the woman who is working at the office talking to the neighbors. She said that the construction work would take a long time because of the lack of workmen. It's an ideal place for your kind."

For Murina, it was clear that only one mouse could have been responsible for this. "The only one that would do something like that is Sori," she said aloud. "She didn't do it alone. She must have had one or more accomplices, but we don't have any evidence."

"Now what?"

"I don't know. After all, I don't fit through mouse holes, so I can't see who is lurking around or what is going on."

Murina looked up at Athena. "I wish I were free so I could find out who was mean to the humans."

"We need to finish our chat; the insects are about to be eaten and I don't want to be seen talking to you." The owl gestured with its beak toward the mouse guard and the prisoners. Murina looked over at the others. "I'll think of something," her friend announced.

Murina felt a breath on the back of her neck, and when she turned around, the owl had disappeared with a soundless flap of wings. She blinked. Had Athena really been here? She quickly rejoined the other prisoners and sought the proximity of her cell neighbor. The mouse prisoners kept walking around, with the guards watching carefully.

Suddenly, footsteps could be heard outside the walls. Murina froze. Was someone coming to the rescue? Did Athena have a plan so soon? She looked up, but the owl wasn't there. Instead, she heard girls' voices.

"Hannah, over here! We'll crawl back through that hole there."

"Wait a minute, Nele, please. I heard something!"

"Typical! There's no one here but us. Every time you make such a fuss. We've been watching the ruin for fifteen minutes, haven't we? Who's supposed to be here?"

"Maybe a few bugs."

The one who was called Hannah giggled nervously.

"As long as no rat runs over my foot," growled the voice that belonged to the human girl Nele.

"I wonder what happened to the mouse from the center?" wondered Hannah. "Now there's no one left to feed it."

"Oh, she'll still be able to crawl around there. I'm sure she'll find something. Your cookie crumbs, for example."

"Haha. You're one to talk! Who's always leaving crumbs?"

Murina's heart was pounding up to her throat. The two girls were talking about her!

"I'd love to know what all the wood slats and tools are doing out here. We'll have to skip math tomorrow and come out here early in the morning."

"Jeez, cut it out! The others are already complaining because we do so much as a couple and sit together all the time."

"Do you think they suspect anything?"

"I don't know. Laura saw me last week when I was biking here. I slipped out that I was going to Citadel Park, and that's when she asked if I had a date with the castle ruins."

Murina heard loud giggling and wondered if humans could really have a date with the ruins. *Strange creatures!*

"Would you mind, then?" asked Nele in a thin voice after a few moments.

"If I had a date with the ruins? I don't get it. A date with the ruins of Sturmstein Castle!"

"That's bullshit. I mean a date with me."

"Not at all! I... really like you."

"Me too. And I couldn't care less what anyone else thinks."

It was quiet for a moment. So quiet that Murina let out a squeak when one of the girls continued unexpectedly enthusiastically, "Come on, let's figure out where and when we're going to set up our Christmas bazaar! Also, you must help me get your last letter out of the cracks in the wall. I can't reach it."

"So far, you've always gotten it. If I help, won't the thrill and sneakiness of it be gone?"

"But what if I absolutely can't get my hands on it?"

"I'm already looking. Here, hold my gloves. Whew, not so easy."

"Are you sure you hid it? It's not on your desk?"

"Yes, I am one hundred percent certain."

"Darn!"

"You finally got it?"

"Don't be so impatient!"

Murina looked amusedly at Sylva, but her cellmate seemed to be scared to death. Her eyes were wide open, and she was shaking all over. And not only her. Everyone around her seemed frozen, including the guard.

Again, footsteps could be heard, and stones of the walls came loose and fell down with a clatter. That was the starting signal.

"Humans into the ruin!" the mouse guard roared, and Murina jumped in fright.

"Everyone inside the cells! Make it snappy!"

"Hurry away!"

"If that's an exterminator..."

"I want to go to my cell!"

The other mice almost ran Murina down, and the mouse guard pushed her inside the ruin. Before she knew it, she was back in the dungeon with Sylva.

For a long time, she struggled with whether to tell Sylva about her owl friend's visit, but soon she fell asleep from sheer exhaustion.

CHAPTER 8 - TROUBLEMAKERS

Ida looked discontentedly at the group of people present, trying to keep her calm and digest what she had just heard.

"You are sure that several people entered the old ruin through the fence at once?"

"Exactly, there were footprints of different sizes. The craftsmen saw them immediately in the snow. Fortunately, nothing seems to have been stolen and there is no damage," confirmed Ms. Singer, the main person responsible for organizing the Christmas Market.

"But what do they want there? Are they homeless people or teenagers looking for a place to smoke pot?"

"We should hire a security guard or put up a camera," Ms. Singer advised.

"I'm okay with anything as long as it doesn't draw attention. No large-scale setup with motion detectors and full lighting. After all, the construction is not yet complete."

Ms. Singer was taking notes on her tablet. "I'll check with a couple of security companies right away to see what capacity they have on site. I'm sure they'll give us a fair quote."

"That sounds good." Ida nodded in agreement. The cooperation with the *FunEvent* company, with which she had jointly organized a whole series of events so far, had always been satisfactory.

"We should have put guards there right from the start. Just too naive of me to think that such a ruin wouldn't attract nosy people," she admitted. "Especially when there's construction going on. It's just a small town and not a tranquil village like Bergfels, where residents don't even have to lock their doors."

"I assumed that the company providing the craftsmen for the booths had at least installed a camera," Ms. Singer justified herself.

"Well, we will get to the bottom of the uninvited visitors. Make sure that surveillance begins today."

CHAPTER 9 – A DREAM OR FORESHADOWING?

Babsi jumped up from the couch. Only slowly did she come back to reality. Her eyes studied the walls of the castle ruins. Walls? Strangely enough, it wasn't stones she saw, but wallpaper...

No. She shook her head. Babsi was not in the ruins, but in her living room. And there was no mouse running around here, was there? Just a moment ago, she had thought she was looking for the mouse, which, dragging a parchment paper behind it, had run away through long ruin corridors.

Babsi took a deep breath and expelled it thoughtfully. Once again, she looked around. Not a creature to be seen far and wide. She must have fallen asleep; the workday had been exhausting. *Why, of all things, does the ruined castle haunt my dreams?*

"Are you okay?" Theodora stuck her head through the door. "Oh, did you fall asleep? Did I wake you up?"

"No, but I actually dozed off and had a crazy nightmare..." A ring at the front door interrupted her.

"Who could that be? Did you invite someone over?" asked Theodora in wonder.

"No, I would have told you that."

"Or did Hannah forget her key?"

"I thought Hannah was already in her room?"

Theodora shook her head in denial.

"Theodora, would you mind answering the door?"

Babsi sat up and rubbed her eyes while her wife left the room. An unannounced visitor? *Unusual.* She heard strange voices from the hallway.

"Barbara? Will you come here, please?" That's what Theodora called her only in serious situations.

"Coming!" Babsi stood up and stepped into the hallway. "Is there a..." She was startled to see Hannah standing in front of the door, flanked by two police officers.

CHAPTER 10 - CAUGHT

"That's really cool, eh, you know the Countess for real? Tell me, how did you meet her? Will you introduce me to her?" Hannah bounced up and down excitedly on the luxury Italian designer sofa. It didn't seem to bother Theodora in any way, although she was usually so meticulous about her furniture.

Frowning, Babsi pushed the Coke glass on the table out of her daughter's reach. Just the thought that she might spill the drink onto the white carpet made her hair stand on end.

The carpet had undoubtedly cost an entire month's salary. She herself would at best have allowed her daughter a glass of tap water after the incident.

In her opinion, the conversation took place in the wrong place, namely in the living room of Theodora's apartment. Her wife normally considered the room her sanctuary and they only used it for special guests.

Babsi would have preferred to have this conversation in her own apartment one floor up. Their parlor was cozier, with worn carpet and a comfortable sofa and armchairs, especially since that was where all three of them spent most of their time together. This would have made her feel more at ease and given her more backbone to be stern with her daughter.

On top of that, the whole thing was going in the completely wrong direction. Theodora was enjoying Hannah's attention far too much. It couldn't go on like this—Babsi had to intervene.

"Hannah, you're not sitting here to question Theodora, you're sitting here because we... because *I* have questions for you, and I want to know what's gotten into you." She tried to get back to the real reason for the conversation. "You've just been taken home by the police for sneaking through the fences of the castle ruins in the park with a friend and fooling around."

"Oh, Ma, we didn't fool around there, such bullshit!" Hannah groaned and rolled her eyes. "Besides, it wasn't just any friend, it was Nele. Calm yourself, we were just hanging out and having a little fun."

"Are you crazy?" Indignantly, Babsi threw her arms in the air. "And you can't have this kind of *fun* anywhere else?"

"It's always so cool out there. The day before yesterday, Nele and I found something there..." Hannah put her hand over her mouth.

"This wasn't your first time at the ruin's terrain?" Babsi was stunned.

"We wanted to think about where we could hold the bazaar as a replacement," Hannah babbled on, ignoring her question. "Tell me how to find a place at the last minute. When people hear the words *Recreational Center for Girls and Young Women* and *Lesbian Line*, they're all booked up at once."

She slumped against the back of the sofa and gasped. Abruptly, she straightened up again. "There are little wooden booths set up all over the front lawn of the ruin, all covered with huge tarps. Something is going on there. It's a pity that everything was locked. Suddenly, guards came, and we had to hide. But they came after us. They wouldn't let us leave; they just *had* to call the police. In all the excitement I also lost my earring."

"It must have been pretty dark inside the old walls," Theodora surmised.

"That's right, it's really creepy, none of us have a location like this to hang out in. The long hallway is so cool and there are so many secret corners to hide in." Hannah gave her mother a dirty look. "There are also no parents to interfere."

"Aside from the fact that you gave me a good scare and caused conversation in the neighborhood with your uniformed companions, you could have gotten hurt! And I don't even want to know what kind of creatures are scurrying around there, apart from mice and rats."

"But they're not doing anything, Mom! Too bad the cops didn't turn on the siren. We couldn't persuade them to drive a little faster or turn on the red and blue lights either," Hannah grumbled. "Nele secretly filmed the drive with her phone. I'm sure she'll post it on the web." Hannah straightened up and squinted over at her phone, placed on the sideboard out of reach. Her mother had taken it from her.

"Don't even think about it!" Babsi growled. "You're going straight to your room after dinner. And you are staying home this weekend! Phone and internet shenanigans are canceled, movies and music as well."

"But then I can't write to Nele," Hannah protested, hastily adding, "And talk to her about homework and exams."

As if her daughter cared about school. Babsi didn't believe a word she said and didn't want to get involved in further conversation or negotiation. "You can save yourself the discussion. It'll give you plenty of time to think about your stupid actions. And if you need a break, there are lots of nice books on the shelf waiting for you to touch and truly read."

***

After dinner, Babsi and Theodora sat in front of the fireplace and talked about what happened.

"I don't know how to thank you for protecting Hannah from the policewomen like that," Babsi said, bravely swallowing down the tears that were gathering in the corners of her eyes. "When they said that they had to notify the owners of the castle ruins and that it was the Count's family, my vision went back for a second."

Theodora gently stroked her back.

"I didn't know until today that the castle ruins were owned by Ida's family."

"Then what you said is true? That you are a good friend of the Count's family? What are their names? Bergfels-thingy, oh, I've got it, Bergfeld-Bloom…"

"Count and Countess of Bergfels-Blumenheide is their name," Theodora corrected, laughing softly. "They also own Bergfels Palace, situated on the verge of Bergfels Village, where we had planned our short vacation."

"I thought you only said this to impress Hannah and get the cops off your back, so they'd leave it at a warning." Babsi shook her head in disbelief. She didn't even like to imagine what kind of consequences the whole thing could cause. What happened in the case of trespassing? Would she have to hire a lawyer? Babsi could literally see her bank account shrinking. She had saved a small amount for the short vacation. Did she need the money now to keep her daughter out of jail? She hated being financially dependent on her wife.

"They're still minors, can they even be punished?"

"They are no longer exempt from punishment," Theodora replied matter-of-factly. "They would fall under the juvenile justice system. Maybe they would have to do some community service."

"Can you call Ida's family and confess to them as gently as possible that this is your stepdaughter?" Babsi looked up at her anxiously.

"Yes, I'll have to do that whether I like it or not. Unless you would like to talk to them?"

Babsi waved her hands defensively. "For heaven's sake, no! They don't know me at all. I don't know how to explain this."

Theodora sighed. "I'd best call Ida tonight."

"Do you think the police have already told them about the incident?"

"It's possible. I need to call Ida and explain that it was Hannah and her friend and there was no malicious intent behind it."

Theodora stood up and picked up her phone from the charging station. "Don't worry about it. I'm sure Ida and her family won't do anything further."

CHAPTER 11 - JEALOUSY

Babsi stood in the kitchen and jingled loudly with the plates. Again and again, she cast a desperate glance into the oven, where the casserole was simmering. Soon the golden-brown crust would burn.

She understood that Theodora didn't often find time to call her friend Ida. But ever since the conversation three days ago, when Hannah had been brought home by the police, she seemed to be constantly on the phone with her aristocratic friend. Babsi had thought the matter would have been settled after Theodora's call, even though her wife had not yet had time to tell her about the details of the conversation.

Not that Babsi was jealous. There was no reason to be. Or was there? She didn't know Ida and should ask Thealein thoroughly about her. Had Theodora and Ida perhaps once been a couple? *Great!*

She took a deep breath. Hannah and her friend Nele were to blame for this. If they hadn't been picked up in the castle ruins, Theodora would certainly have no reason to chat with this Countess so often. Babsi looked down at her baggy sweatshirt and plush slippers that adorned her feet. Ida probably wore only high-end brands at home, too. Just like Theodora. She gulped. Babsi could hardly keep up with someone like that.

She puffed out her cheeks. Indecisively, she looked at the set kitchen table. Her stomach growled loudly. Should she take the plates and set them down with a bang on the dining room table where her wife was talking on the phone? Drop another fork? Or shout loudly across the hall that dinner was ready?

But wasn't Ida married? Although that was no guarantee.

"Oh, Babsi, you jealous thing," she scolded herself. Annoyed by her absurd train of thought, she reached with pointed fingers for the letter Hannah and Nele had found in the castle ruins. Shyly, Hannah had confessed to her that she and Nele secretly wrote letters to each other and hid them in the cracks in the walls inside the castle. Hannah's descriptions had revealed her admiration for her athletic friend. Her daughter and Nele seemed to be developing feelings for each other, Babsi suspected. She just couldn't be mad at

Hannah any longer, even if she didn't approve of her loitering around the castle ruins.

In any case, one of Hannah's letters had slipped so far into the masonry that Nele had only been able to reach for it with difficulty. In the process, she had pulled out this old paper with almost indecipherable handwriting.

Since the old letter was hard to decipher, but Hannah and Nele really wanted to know what was in it, Hannah had shown it to her. The paper was stained and torn at the corners, if not eaten by mice or other animals. Some of the ink was smudged so that the writing was barely legible.

Goosebumps ran down Babsi's spine. She reflected back to the nightmare she had a few days ago, in which a mouse and a letter had appeared. Had that been a premonition?

Babsi squinted her eyes and tried to decipher what was written. It read, *Princess* and *feithfulli.* How strangely people had spoken and written in the past! Strained she looked at the writing, but besides *my wyrd, my doom,* she couldn't decipher anything else. A professional had to be called in.

"What have you got there?" Theodora brought her out of her musings.

"My God, you scared me! Are you finally through with your phone call?"

"Postponed. Ida has an appointment and..."

"Fine," Babsi interrupted her wife, setting the paper aside, "then we can eat at last. Do you want to call her downstairs?" She didn't even want to know why Ida didn't have any more time. She couldn't care less.

She took the casserole out of the oven and spread the food on the plates.

"Hey, leave some for me," Hannah grumbled as she entered the kitchen and squeakily pulled back her chair.

"I only now realize how hungry I am." Theodora lowered the cutlery and made no effort to devote herself to the food.

"Hannah, I have something to discuss with you and Babsi after dinner," she announced instead with a serious face. "But your mother has made such an effort with the cooking, that we shouldn't let the casserole get cold."

Babsi couldn't enjoy the casserole, thinking all the while about what her wife was about to announce that was so important. No sooner had Hannah and Theodora finished the last bite than she pulled the empty plates from under them and put them in the dishwasher.

"What do you want to talk to us about? Should we stay here or go to the living room?" With her arms folded, Babsi leaned against the sideboard.

"No, we can discuss it here, it won't take long. I must keep working after this," Theodora explained. "Well, it's like this: The Count doesn't want Hannah and her friend to go completely unpunished because of their trip to the castle ruins. I've asked Ida to speak to him several times, but he won't budge. For him, he says, this is a lesson."

Babsi put her hand over her mouth. She had suspected it! How could she have been so naive and assumed that there would be no consequences? Surely the Count's family had a whole armada of lawyers who had advised her to report the two girls.

There was a look of horror on Hannah's face.

"Do Nele and I have to go to jail now?" She was completely pale and stared at Theodora with wide-open eyes.

"Should I get a lawyer?" Babsi felt sorry for her daughter. The young girls simply hadn't been thinking when they had entered the ruin. But to turn them in for it? She was all wobbly on her feet. Babsi pulled up a chair and sat down again.

"No, that won't be necessary," Theodora reassured her, giving her a gentle smile. "But," she turned to Hannah, "you and Nele should formally apologize to the Count. He will also expect something in return. Sit down together as soon as possible and write a letter. Let me look over it afterward, though. I don't want him to have a heart attack because of all possible spelling mistakes you could make."

Babsi sighed with relief. That didn't sound like a criminal charge. An idea occurred to her. "Maybe Hannah and Nele have also discovered something that the Count might like." Encouragingly, she nodded to her daughter.

"What do you mean?" asked Hannah perplexed, but her expression cleared up after a few seconds and she seemed to guess her mother's thoughts. "You mean the letter?"

"Exactly."

"What letter?" asked Theodora. "Oh, you're talking about the ancient-looking letter you just read?" She looked from Babsi to Hannah with interest.

"We can't read it, and Mom can't decipher the writing either."

"Who is 'we?'"

"Nele and me. We found it in the castle ruins. It's really ancient, almost falling apart and totally stained."

"Surely someone left this letter as a joke," Theodora surmised. "A letter like that doesn't just lie around in a ruin for years."

"It wasn't just lying around. Nele pulled it out of the walls."

Babsi saw Hannah blush and stroked her arm briefly.

"We write letters to each other and hide them there in the cracks in the walls. Nele started doing that a few weeks ago and put a trail there for me."

Theodora raised her eyebrows. "I won't ask why you hide letters in a ruin in the age of the Internet and e-mails, when smartphones have practically grown on you," she said dryly and went to the sideboard where the letter lay.

"He sure looks old," she noted. "I think I'll have to put my work on hold."

Babsi and her daughter looked at each other, puzzled.

"It's just paperwork waiting for me anyway." Theodora waved it off. "Well, let's try to decipher it together, or at least determine what ancient writing it is. Hannah, would you get my reading glasses from the living room, please?"

As soon as Hannah disappeared from the kitchen, Babsi got up and went to her wife. "Thank you." She breathed a kiss on Theodora's cheek.

"For what?"

"For putting your work aside and helping us decipher this letter."

CHAPTER 12 – THE VERDICT

Murina was trembling all over her body. Today was the day when the trial resumed. Even though rumors of all kinds circulated in the prison, she hadn't heard a peep about the crime scene from the otherwise amazingly well-informed prisoners.

It was crowded in the courtroom, with Sori and her friends in attendance again. *No,* she corrected herself, *there is only one companion at Sori's side.* Were they at odds?

"Silence, please!" Judge Arvalis' voice rang out. She struck the judge's desk in front of her with a hazelnut and the murmuring died away.

"After a detailed walk-through of the crime scene and the testimony of another witness..." Murina looked up at her public defender in astonishment. Another witness? "...whose plausible explanations I can fully endorse in my own conviction, I pronounce the following verdict in the name of the Mouse Folks: the defendant Murina is acquitted."

It was as quiet as a mouse in the courtroom.

"The written reasons for the sentence will be sent to the public defender by bat mail before the start of the next lunar phase."

The judge looked over at Sori and her companion with a stern expression on his face. "No appeal is allowed. I order Murina's immediate release. The costs of the proceedings are to be charged to the treasury of the Mouse State." Arvalis gestured toward the guards, who briskly surrounded the two shrews.

"Mouse Sori, in return, I order an immediate arrest for you and your companion. You are suspected of damaging the electrical wiring in the *Recreational Center for Girls and Young Women*."

"Objection!" exclaimed Sori. "We only used the cables for dental care to keep our teeth short and sharp!"

But Arvalis was not impressed by this and continued with a raised voice, "You have damaged the electrical lines in the center in order to take possession of it. Furthermore, there are witnesses who have observed you dragging cheese scraps, pieces of fruit, cleaning rags, and remnants of electronic supply lines out of the center. In addition, a dead shrew was found with cable remnants around its neck—the same cables that have been cut. Extraneous fault is to be assumed."

***

Two hours later, Murina and her public defender sat behind a hedge in the garden of the center and listened to Athena's account of the events that had transpired after the judge had inspected the crime scene.

"I slid down out of my favorite tree, intercepted the judge, and told her that you had committed the crime but had already made amends afterwards."

Athena puffed out her feathers a little and, thanks to her plumage, blended in with the surroundings. She continued with her report only after looking around.

"I told her that you were brave enough to show yourself to the young women in the office of the *Recreational Center for Girls and Young Women* at that time, and that they curiously followed you to the trash can."

Murina nodded. That was exactly what had happened. After she had learned by eavesdropping that it was a wanted lottery ticket, she had to get the piece of paper back somehow. "And the judge believed you?"

"She was skeptical at first, but..."

"But that wasn't the end of the story?" the public defender surmised.

"I told her about your death-defying jump into the box," Athena continued. Murina still felt queasy when she thought about the incident.

"Judge Arvalis admired your fearlessness. And when she heard you pulled out the lottery ticket, and the young women later used it to claim a lottery win, she noted to me that it was tantamount to your rehabilitation."

Murina was overjoyed that her friend had stood by her and convinced the judge. "There's one more thing you have to tell me," she turned to Athena. "How could you be sure that it was actually Sori and her friends who gnawed through the cables?"

"I wasn't." Athena winked at her. "But the judge and I were present when the shrew and her accomplices sneaked out of the center with walnuts, rags, and cable scraps. They were arguing, probably because of the walk-through of the crime scene. This was reason enough for the judge to have the premises examined more closely a second time. The rat task force also found the mouse corpse with the cables around its neck."

"Sori knew that Arvalis was going to show up for the crime scene. Why was she hanging around there at the same time? I wouldn't have thought she was that stupid."

"No, not the same day." Athena shook her head contemptuously. "Along with your public defender, I persuaded Judge Arvalis to show up there again the day after the committal and join me here in the bush. I told her I had an idea of who was behind it, but the one is unlikely to show up when the judge is known to be doing a site visit."

"Exactly!" the lawyer interfered triumphantly. "I already reminded Arvalis after the first day of the trial that even in case of the slightest doubt and according to section 242 CCM..." she started, but Athena interrupted her.

"Whatever! Anyway, the next morning there were suddenly walnuts in the office. I saw them lying there through the window as I flew a lap around the center. I dropped the info purely by accident as Sori was scurrying around under my favorite tree. It was the perfect bait for the shrews, just too tempting."

Murina blinked at her friend in disbelief. "There's no one in the building right now, is there?

Since the electricity isn't working? Where did the walnuts come from?" Then it dawned on her. "Did you have something to do with it?"

Athena looked embarrassed all at once. "No, I'm not a squirrel. But maybe I know one that always diligently snatches some from a garden a few houses away."

"You hired a squirrel to put walnuts there? I would like to have your ideas."

"It wasn't an assignment. I was just dropping a few hints. But now we've talked enough about it."

"What's happening with the electrical lines?"

"I've heard that the repair work won't start until January."

"What a pity the Christmas bazaar can't take place," Murina lamented. "I would have loved to have grabbed something tasty for us there. I told you about the colorful hustle and bustle and singing." She held up her little paw and showed a glittery object. "Here, I found this in the ruins when I was making my way home. I think it belongs to one of the girls from the rec center, whom I listened to behind the ruins walls a few days ago."

"Oh, how beautiful!" the public defender exclaimed.

Athena agreed with her. "A pretty gem."

"Only... How am I supposed to return it, with the bazaar not happening and it still being a while before the center can be entered again?"

"I'm sure Athena will have a solution for this, too, right?" the public defender speculated.

"Give me time to think." For the rest of the evening, the owl kept a deep silence.

CHAPTER 13 – MOSAIC BRICKS

"She is quite good and has cried with me," Charlotte read aloud. "And whether my *drerinesse*– uh, that means sadness..." She stopped and tapped a dark spot on the paper with her gloved finger. "Here the ink is so smudged that we can't decipher it. But the next lines are clearly legible again." She held the letter against the light and Ida peered over her shoulder.

"The good princess Agatha shows me all *godnesse,* kindness, so that I love her dearly," Charlotte finished her transcription of the letter of Countess Ernestine of Sturmstein Castle, which she found out had been written at the end of the 17th century.

"Wait, there is another PS in which the Countess emphasizes that she 'cannot *leven*,' that is to say, 'trust everything to the post.'"

"I must admit, the girls found a real treasure in the ruins. You have certainly had the letter checked for authenticity?" inquired Ida's father, the Count of Bergfels-Blumenheide.

"Of course. Otherwise, I wouldn't have taken the trouble to transcribe the letter," she assured her father-in-law. "I contacted three specialists in the early modern period and a medievalist and asked for their assessment, because at first I couldn't place the letter precisely in terms of time. It was only late that Ida discovered a date."

That was her cue, and Ida nodded. "It was cleverly worked into our ancestor's signature with a multitude of squiggles. In fact, while researching our archives, Charlotte discovered two other letters that indicate the close friendship between the Countess and the Princess. Neither of them ever married, although the pressure must have been exceptional. As a marriage would have given their families access to the great palaces of the world. In any case, there was no shortage of suitors. This letter was just the piece of the mosaic, the proof of their love for each other, that was missing."

Her father grinned. "So, you, Flordelis," he usually called Ida by her first name, "are not the first in the family to have reached out to a woman and shared her bed."

Of course, the Count cleverly avoided calling his ancestor or daughter a lesbian.

Ida pushed the thought aside and put a finger under her chin. "It would be too bad if the letter were to languish in our archives. We could present it to the public there after the renovation of Sturmstein Castle."

"And we should definitely make a print of the letter available to local schools! That would be something exciting for German or history classes," Charlotte suggested. "It will definitely be fun for the students to decipher the letter and learn about life in the castle."

A glow came over Ida's face and her father nodded. "That's a great idea."

CHAPTER 14 – GUESSING GAME

It was maddening. Two days ago, Babsi had packed a whole armada of walnut cookies in bags and filled the cookie jar to the brim, but today the content seemed to have shrunk in a strange way. Involuntarily, she had to think of the walnuts that had disappeared from Theodora's garden. A small squirrel had turned out to be the thief back then. Had Theodora taken a few bags of cookies to work?

She shook her head. No, normally Thealein would have asked first instead of just helping herself to the festively wrapped cookies. She had to ask Hannah if she had taken a batch of the bags to school. If she was ever home and responsive and didn't disappear straight to her room. She hadn't been able to get anything out of the child in the last few days. *How strange.*

Babsi would have liked to know what punishment the Count's family had come up with for Nele and her daughter! A good two-thirds of the voluntary work to make amends demanded by the Count had passed. Babsi had actually thought that her daughter would be a little more communicative.

"It was exhausting. The Countess is quite nice, but I'm tired and just want to sleep." Hannah growled like that every time she finished her work.

No word of indignation escaped her lips, no grumbling. What kind of work was this that had been imposed on her daughter?

CHAPTER 15 – DAMN GENEROUS

Thick snowflakes were trickling onto the walls of Sturmstein Castle and Babsi would have preferred to stay at home. The drive through the snowy streets was an adventure and all the people in town seemed to be drawn to Citadel Park and the castle ruins at the same time. There were hardly any parking spaces left.

"Usually, I'm the one who doesn't want to leave the house," Theodora noted.

"I just can't imagine that the Christmas Market in front of the castle ruins can compete with the one at Bergfels Palace. Who organized this one anyway? Don't be angry with me, but I'm sure that this one will not be a compensation for our canceled trip to Bergfels. I'm firmly convinced there are just two huts with cheap mulled wine and a bunch of men from the soccer club gathered around them."

"Now, don't be so pessimistic. You'd better help me carry my photography equipment."

"You're sure this stuff is worth lugging around?"

Reluctantly, Babsi grabbed one of the camera bags. She scowled at the snowy path to avoid slipping and stumbled after her wife. Theodora was already running with wide striding steps in the direction of the castle ruins. Abruptly, she stopped.

"Whew! What's wrong now? Can't you..." Babsi grumbled at it, but fell silent when she turned her gaze to the front.

Many small wooden booths stood decorated for Christmas on the forecourt. A string quartet and two horn players were tuning their instruments in a shelter. They had placed themselves in front of a heater, probably to protect the instruments from the cold. From a small hut the smell of roasted almonds, chestnuts, and mulled wine was wafting over to them.

"First class." Theodora turned to her wife. "Just incredible what Ida has come up with, isn't it? And look how the castle is lit up!"

Shimmering yellowish light made the ruin shine. A few weeks ago, Babsi had dreamed of sitting at a table behind the walls of Sturmstein, and now everything seemed so wonderfully alive! Her bad mood had vanished.

"Theodora!" am excited voice called out. "We're here!"

"Ida! Charlotte!" Beaming with joy, her wife hurried toward the two women, pulling Babsi behind her.

"Babsi, may I introduce you? This is Ida and Charlotte."

Was Theodora really talking about *Ida*? About her friend of many years, who was also a Countess and whose family owned these castle ruins?

Babsi was a little disappointed when she eyed the Countess. She was dressed in what must have been an expensive but simple-looking parka and her ears were covered with a self-knitted headband, which somehow looked familiar to Babsi.

"Hello," she greeted the two women with the friendliest smile possible. "How nice to finally meet you in person." She shook their hands and eyed the pair.

I should have put on my winter coat and not come here in this old down jacket, she thought.

"Look what I bought at Hannah and Nele's booth!" Ida turned in a circle and plucked at the edge of the headband as if it were a noble hat.

"Hannah and Nele?" Babsi looked around in amazement. "They're here, too? I thought they were on their way to some out-of-town Christmas market?"

Theodora nodded and seemed thievishly pleased. "That's right. Out of town in the sense of... on the outskirts of town at the castle ruins. With her friends and a few women from the rec center. Ida has provided them with a small hut and two covered stalls for their bazaar items."

"There in the corner, let's go to her," Ida followed up.

"But that's damn noble. It's not really punitive work that your father has put the girls through," Babsi remarked.

"Damn generous of him," Theodora confirmed.

"Let's just say that bringing in and setting up the decorations and some of the items for sale was definitely an energy-sapping task for the girls and no walk in the park " Ida winked. "On top of that, they had to take turns looking after their stalls."

"They shouldn't tell you about it and should keep it a secret." Theodora wrung her hands. "When I talked to Ida on the phone after the girls' trip, she told me about her plans to hold a Christmas fair here. But I wanted to keep it a surprise, at least for you."

"You planned and organized all this and hid it from me?" Babsi's heart warmed. "I didn't suspect a thing. Oh my God, I could hug all of you."

"Now, let's go!" urged Theodora. "They're already waiting."

Babsi didn't have to be asked twice and quickly they reached the small hut where her daughter and Nele were standing behind a table with self-made candlesticks, knitted gloves, and headbands as well as stones painted with Christmas motifs.

"Surprise!" they called out to them and Babsi rubbed her eyes in wonder. Her daughter was jumping up and down excitedly like a little girl.

Curious, Babsi marveled at the items on the table. The walnut cookies sold in small transparent bags looked remarkably similar to the ones she had baked last weekend. She had to admit that they were exquisitely presented behind a decorative plate of nuts and crafted paper stars.

"Just look!" exclaimed Nele.

"Ha! There! I told you: the mouse is here." Hannah pointed to a small crack in the wooden hut.

Theodora immediately stepped closer. "Oh yes, indeed."

Babsi could have run away screaming. But in no case did she want to show her fear in front of all the people at the Christmas Market.

"Are those really mouse ears peeking out of the gap?" asked Charlotte curiously. "With all this going on?"

Hannah and Nele cackled away, and Theodora nudged Babsi with a teasing smile.

"Honey, you should see your face. As if any mice would show up in this crowd of people."

"Mom, really? You believed us?"

With all the happy faces around her, Babsi couldn't be angry. Even if she thought she had seen a small figure scurrying away. But before she could comment, Nele tugged excitedly at Hannah's sleeve.

"I'm going crazy! Do you see what's down there?" With that, she drew everyone's attention to the floor and Babsi's daughter let out a soft cry.

"My earring! How did it get here?"

"It was probably buried somewhere in your jacket pocket and fell out," Babsi guessed, thinking about the things she had fished out of her daughter's pockets before doing laundry.

Charlotte and Ida nodded to each other. "Hannah, Nele, can your friends keep an eye on the booth for a moment? We want to show you something."

"Sure," Hannah replied. "Is there anywhere else you'd like us to help?"

"No, come with me!" Ida said, while asking Babsi and Theodora to join them. They walked to a canopy where there was a glass box. Next to it was a man in security clothing.

"We have another surprise." Charlotte pointed to a letter inside the glass box.

Hannah's jaw dropped.

"This is the letter we found in the castle."

"Do you see that next to it? Someone must have been able to read that." Enthusiastically, Nele pointed her finger at a transcription of the text.

"Wait, I'll take a picture of it."

"You don't have to." Charlotte pressed a small booklet into each girl's hand. "You can read the contents of the letter at your leisure later."

But the two friends had long since opened the pages and skimmed the lines. Hannah looked over at Nele with red cheeks.

"It seems that two friends used to write each other and put letters in wall cracks many years ago," she speculated.

"No." Charlotte laughed out. "It wasn't quite like that, but you can find out for yourself."

"I got it: they had a date with the castle's ruins," Babsi heard her daughter whisper in Nele's ear.

"If anything, it's the *castle*," Nele replied softly. "I guess it wasn't a ruin back then."

Babsi didn't want to listen or stare. Not really. She didn't begrudge the friends—who made a truly cute couple—the intimate moment, and the joy over the find they had made in the ruin. Nevertheless, she looked into her daughter's eyes and couldn't turn away fast enough. Hannah had not missed her mother's eavesdropping and glances. Hastily, she moved away from Nele and waved the little booklet around busily.

"Mom, can you take this home before it disappears here? The market goes on until the evening, doesn't it?" Hannah held the gift out to her mother.

"Yes, please, Ms. Foehr, can you take mine, too?" joined Nele.

"Wait, wait, let me take another picture of you and the letter. Ida, will you stand with them? The fact that two girls found a noblewoman's letter in our castle ruins will make a wonderful anecdote for my story." Skillfully, Theodora placed her models around the displayed document and snapped them from several angles.

"Oh my, I think we should really help Emilia and Laura now," Nele remarked as soon as Theodora had finished taking pictures. She pointed to the other friends at their booth. "Look how many people are standing in front of our crafts." Again, she jiggled Hannah's arm. "There's a good crowd. And Luna is looking over at us all worried-like."

"Go ahead. I'll come by your booth later and take the booklets with me. Your friends could use some help, don't keep them waiting," Babsi advised the girls, who were now hurrying back to their buddies.

"I'll get us all mulled wine and you look for a seat on the benches," Ida suggested. "In a moment my father will give the opening speech and then the musicians will begin their concert."

A while later they enjoyed the warm drink, applauded the Count after his entertaining greeting to the numerous guests, and listened to the Christmas carols. At the end of the small concert, the artists played *Silent Night* and most of the audience hummed along softly.

Babsi snuggled up to Theodora and whispered in her ear, "Even though I don't know Ida's hometown... this is at least as nice as a vacation in Bergfels. I take back what I said earlier about our Christmas market."

"Do you remember our walk here a few weeks ago?"

"Yeah. Why?"

"There, too, you said something you need to correct." Theodora smirked. "Or are you still firmly convinced that no drama has taken place behind the walls of Sturmstein Castle?"

"You're right," Babsi admitted. "The letter Hannah and Nele found is proof that something like this must have happened here."

***

Behind a crevice in the wall of the castle ruins squatted Murina and Athena. A torn bag of walnut cookies lay in front of them, and they enjoyed the lively activity.

They sat far enough away to protect their sensitive ears from the high-pitched sounds of the stringed instruments, but if Murina strained hard enough, she could hear the fearsome roar of the prison guards quite distantly, from the depths of the walls.

The memories of her time in the ruins would stay with her forever. But up here, next to her owl friend, she felt safe and secure. The tantalizing scents wafting over and the delicious cookies she had nimbly procured from the girls' stall made up for all the bad times.

She was fortified for all the tasks and events that awaited her at the *Recreational Center for Girls and Young Women*. Even if it was only to track down a lost earring.

ACKNOWLEDGEMENT

This volume could not have been published without the help of my loyal test readers Stefanie and Uschi and my wife, Petra.

Senta Herrmann completed the editing and proofreading for the German version of this story, which allowed my manuscript to transform into a readable short story.

The reliable and competent Sierra Campbell made all the necessary adjustments and corrections to my English translation. Dear Sierra, you did a lot of proofreading and were extremely sensitive when polishing the manuscript.

I can't thank you all enough!

***

I would also like to say a big thank you to everyone who has followed the adventures of my characters since I published the first short story.

***

If you liked this short story, I would love for you to leave a rating or review on one of the numerous platforms!

Contact: Claudine-Auteur@web.de

ALSO BY CLAUDIA HAASE

What's Christmas Without Walnut Cookies?

Theodora wanted to spend the lead-up to the holidays and Christmas Eve quietly at home. Alone. But everything turns out differently, because her new tenant moved in with her teenage daughter at the end of November. And from then on, Theodora's highly appreciated walnuts suddenly disappear from the terrace. Who could be responsible for this?

The mother and teenager seem to celebrate the pre-Christmas season extensively. At that point, Theodora realized she must get rid of them as quickly as possible. But soon after she became involved in their daily lives, more than she could ever have imagined.

Paperback, 48 pages, ISBN-10: 375684448X
ISBN-13: 978-3756844487

Christmas at Bergfels Palace

Charlotte Weinhold has a degree in history and is striving to complete her Ph.D. Her earnings from a newspaper job keep her just above water. When the editor-in-chief demands insider news about the Count of Bergfels-Blumenheide and his family, on whom she is writing her dissertation, she sees this as an opportunity to obtain previously unpublished documents at the same time.

Arriving in Bergfels, she unexpectedly gets a job in the only café in town – its owner is not only attractive but also happens to be the best friend of the Count's publicity-shy daughter. What a unique opportunity to get the desired internal information about the Count's family without much effort!

Countess Ida doesn't care about her title. She lives in a city apartment and works for a non-profit children's aid organization. When her father asks her to take over an archival tour of Bergfels Palace in his place, she agrees. In return, this gives her an excuse to spend the approaching Christmas holidays away from the Count's clan.

But everything turns out quite differently than either Charlotte or Ida could ever have imagined.

Paperback, 96 pages, ISBN: 978-3-7578-2943-8

IN GERMAN LANGUAGE:

Walnussplätzchen unterm Weihnachtsbaum (2020)

Athena und Murina. Eine vorweihnachtliche Geschichte rund um das Lesbenberatungstelefon im Kulturhaus für Frauen und Mädchen (2020)

Weihnachten im Schloss (2021)

Rendezvous mit einer Burgruine (2022)

Eine treue Gesellin mir zur Seite (Arbeitstitel, 2024)